HAVE YOU EVER HEARD OF A

Snotgoblin?

Emily Fell

ROGUE GIRAFFE
BOOKS

First published by Nightingale Books imprint of Pegasus Elliott Mackenzie Publisher Ltd. in 2024
This edition in 2024 by Rogue Giraffe Books

Rogue Giraffe Books Ltd
www.roguegiraffebooks.co.uk

A CIP catalogue record for this title is available from the British Library.

ISBN 978-1-7390940-0-3

ROGUE GIRAFFE
BOOKS

For James, Violet and Gabriella.
May your sniffles never last long!

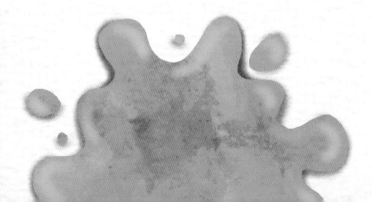

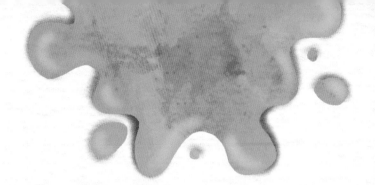

When you're full of sniffles,
And a cold is on its way,
Have you ever wondered,
What helps it go away?

You're tired and you're shivering,
But yet you're boiling hot.
Your nose is a constant drip,
Of yucky, oozing snot.

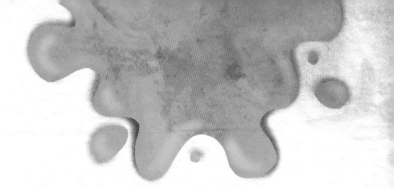

"Off to bed with you" Mum says,
And tucks you up all tight.
But even Mum is unaware,
Of what goes on at night.

When you've finally closed your eyes,
And have drifted off to sleep,
A creature called a Snotgoblin,
Comes out and has a peep!

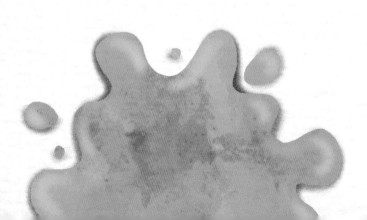

SPINNING HEAD

Their head can spin all the way round to make sure they don't miss any tasty snot!

BIG SQUARE EARS

Their ears are big and square to help scrape off all the snot stuck up your nose – a bit like a shovel!

SQUISHY BODY

Their body is all squishy so they can fit into the smallest of noses by changing shape!

STRETCHY ARMS

Their arms are super stretchy to help reach snot stuck right up your nose – yuck!

BIG FLIPPER FEET

Their big feet are full of bounce and help them jump right up your nose!

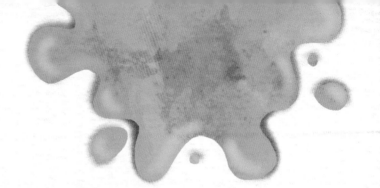

They're green and they're squishy,
And they really are quite small.
In fact you'd never see one,
As they're less than one inch tall.

No need to be afraid though,
These creatures are your friend.
They just want what's up your nose,
To make your bad cold end.

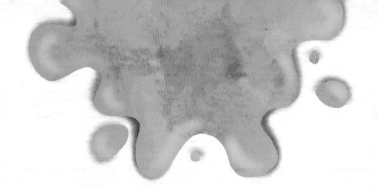

You see their favourite thing is snot –
Sticky, green and grim.
They pick it out from up your nose,
And fill up on it to the brim.

To us, snot is a horrible, foul,
And treacherous slime.
But to a hungry Snotgoblin,
Fresh snot is just divine!

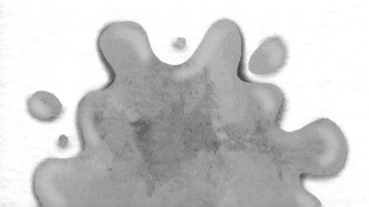

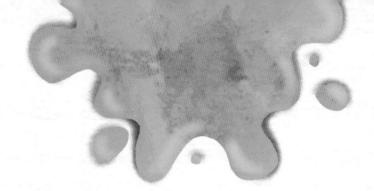

Their stretchy arms and flipper feet,
Come in handy when it's time,
To get right up your nostrils –
To them it's quite a climb!

Just one big bounce is all it takes,
For them to hop inside.
They hang on to your nose hair,
And up your nose they glide.

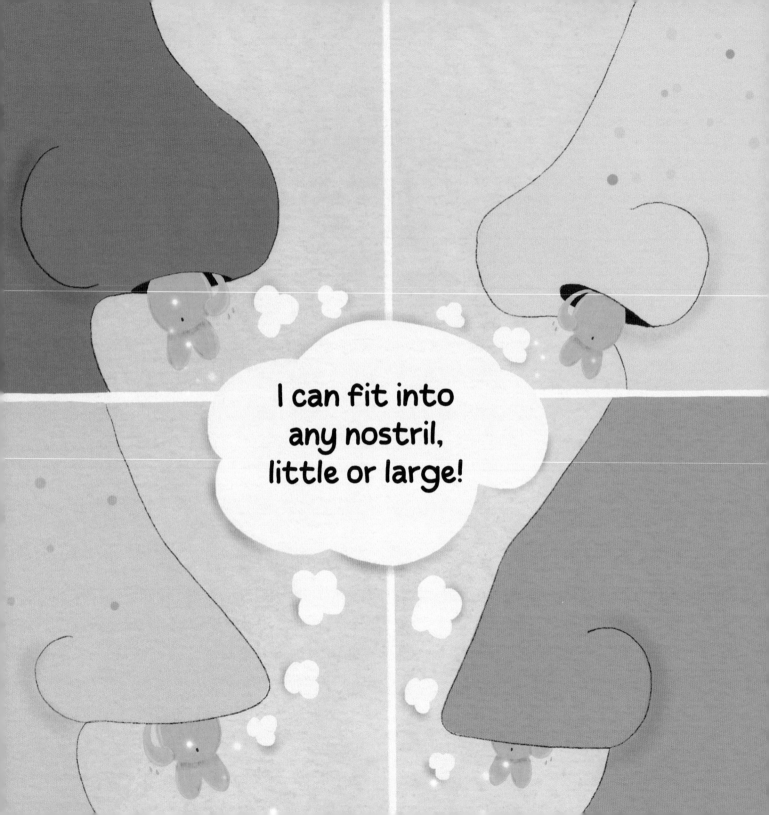

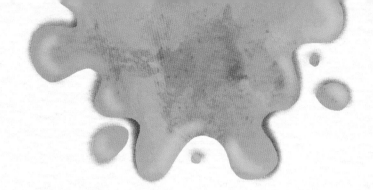

Their squishy body works a treat,
To squeeze through any gap.
But you won't feel anything,
Whilst you take your nap.

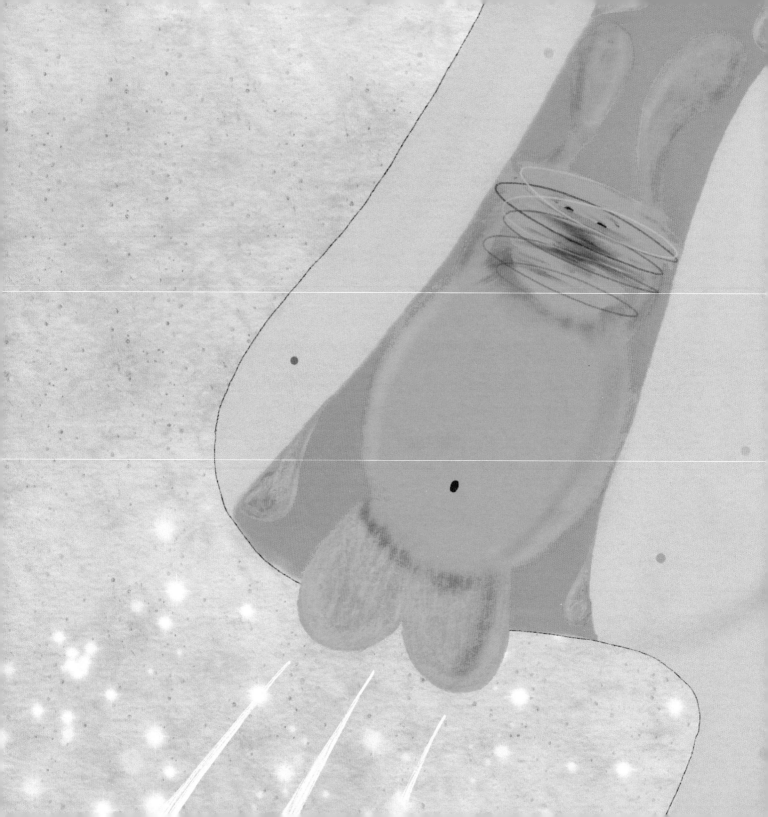

Once they're in they use their head,
They turn it round and round.
This scrapes off all the snot,
Without making a sound.

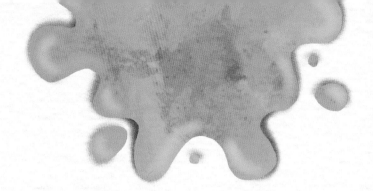

When your nostrils are all clear,
And the Snotgoblin has had its fill,
It scurries off from where it came,
Just beneath the windowsill.

Morning comes and up you get,
Are you ready for the day?
Of course you are, you're fighting fit,
Your cold's been taken away!

Printed in Great Britain
by Amazon